HOW IT WORKS

WI-FI

by Janet Slingerland

FOCUS READERS

FOCUS READERS

WWW.FOCUSREADERS.COM

Focus Readers is distributed by North Star Editions:
sales@northstareditions.com | 888-417-0195

Produced for Focus Readers by Red Line Editorial.

Content Consultant: Dr. Sherali Zeadally, Associate Professor, College of Communication and Information, University of Kentucky

Photographs ©: pawel_p/iStockphoto, cover, 1; cofotoisme/iStockphoto, 4–5; monkeybusinessimages/iStockphoto, 6, 14–15, 22–23; ymgerman/iStockphoto, 9; Xurzon/iStockphoto, 10–11; ttsz/iStockphoto, 12; viach80/iStockphoto, 17; ronen/iStockphoto, 18; JaCZhou/iStockphoto, 21; arka38/Shutterstock Images, 25; xijian/iStockphoto, 26–27; Peter Gercke/dpa/picture-alliance/Newscom, 28

ISBN
978-1-63517-240-9 (hardcover)
978-1-63517-305-5 (paperback)
978-1-63517-435-9 (ebook pdf)
978-1-63517-370-3 (hosted ebook)

Library of Congress Control Number: 2017935928

Printed in the United States of America
Mankato, MN
June, 2017

ABOUT THE AUTHOR

Before writing children's books, Janet Slingerland was an engineer. She programmed computers that went in things such as telephones and submarines. Janet lives in New Jersey with her husband, three children, and a dog.

TABLE OF CONTENTS

CHAPTER 1

GOING WIRELESS

People access the Internet from many different places. Families stream movies in their living rooms. Students check their e-mail between classes. Travelers read the news between flights at airports.

Before Wi-Fi, information on the Internet was sent using wires or cables.

Wi-Fi networks allow people to share information across short distances without using wires.

Tablets, laptops, and smartphones are only some of the devices that can use Wi-Fi.

People could use the Internet only on devices that plugged into these cables. Wi-Fi uses radio waves instead of wires to send information. This allows people to connect to the Internet on the go. All they need is a device that can send and receive the radio waves.

The Federal Communications Commission (FCC) is a US government agency. It controls who can **broadcast** radio waves in the United States. The FCC gives users **licenses** to use certain radio-wave bands. In 1985, the FCC freed a few of the radio-wave bands. People no longer needed a license to use these bands. The bands were called junk bands.

A few companies began making devices that used the junk bands. The devices could send and receive information. But there was a problem. The companies used different communication methods. Devices made by one company could not communicate with devices made by a different company.

In 1988, the Institute of Electrical and Electronics Engineers (IEEE) started work on a **standard** that all wireless devices would use. The standard was finally released in 1997. It was known as 802.11. All companies made devices that followed this standard. As a result, devices from different companies could work together. This gave users easy access to wireless connections.

However, IEEE 802.11 was not a very catchy name. In 1999, companies chose a new name for the standard. They called it Wi-Fi. This name was inspired by Hi-Fi, or high fidelity. Hi-Fi describes high-quality music, pictures, or videos.

Hotels often offer free Wi-Fi to guests.

Wi-Fi's popularity grew during the 2000s. Many people used it to connect their home computers to the Internet. Today, people often use Wi-Fi with devices such as smartphones or tablets. Many schools, restaurants, and other public places have Wi-Fi networks.

CHAPTER 2

RADIO WAVES

Wi-Fi uses radio waves to send information. Radio waves are a form of electromagnetic (EM) radiation. EM radiation is light that moves as a wave. Imagine a rock that is dropped in a pond. Ripples move out from the point where the rock hits the water. The ripples look like circles around that point.

Radio waves are often sent through the air by antennas.

EM radiation is also a kind of wave. Visible light is one type of EM wave. But there are many other kinds, including radio waves. Most EM waves are not visible.

Radio waves are used to send and receive many kinds of information. Radio

THE EM SPECTRUM

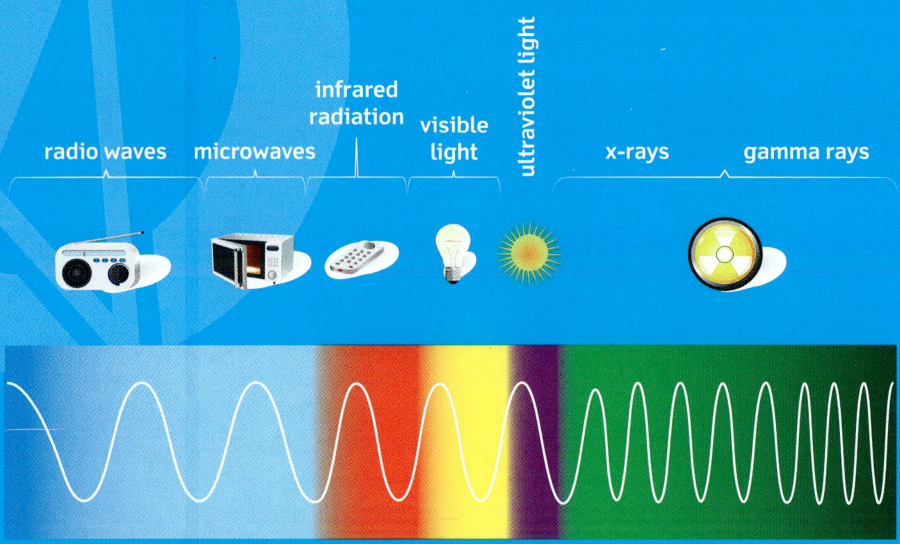

stations use them to transmit music. Radio waves can also be used to control model cars and planes.

There are many kinds of radio waves. Each kind is defined by its **frequency**. Frequency is measured in units called hertz. A wave that has one cycle per second has a frequency of one hertz. The junk bands that Wi-Fi uses have frequencies of 900 **megahertz**, 2.4 **gigahertz**, and 5.8 gigahertz.

CRITICAL THINKING

What are some other devices or inventions that use waves from the EM spectrum?

CHAPTER 3

SENDING SIGNALS

The way Wi-Fi devices send and receive radio waves is similar to the process used by radio stations. First, a radio station converts music into radio waves. Then the station broadcasts those waves. A radio picks up the waves. It translates the waves back into music. The music comes out of the radio's speakers.

Text messages, photos, and e-mail messages can all be sent through the air using Wi-Fi technology.

Wi-Fi devices also send and receive radio waves. But instead of carrying music, the radio waves carry **data**. First, the device converts the data into radio waves. Then the device's **transmitter** sends the radio waves out. Another device's **receiver** picks up the radio waves and changes them back into data.

Each Wi-Fi device has a radio antenna. The antenna picks up incoming signals. It also sends out signals. Some Wi-Fi devices have just one antenna. Other devices have many antennas. There are different kinds of antennas. The antenna may be inside the device, or it may stick out.

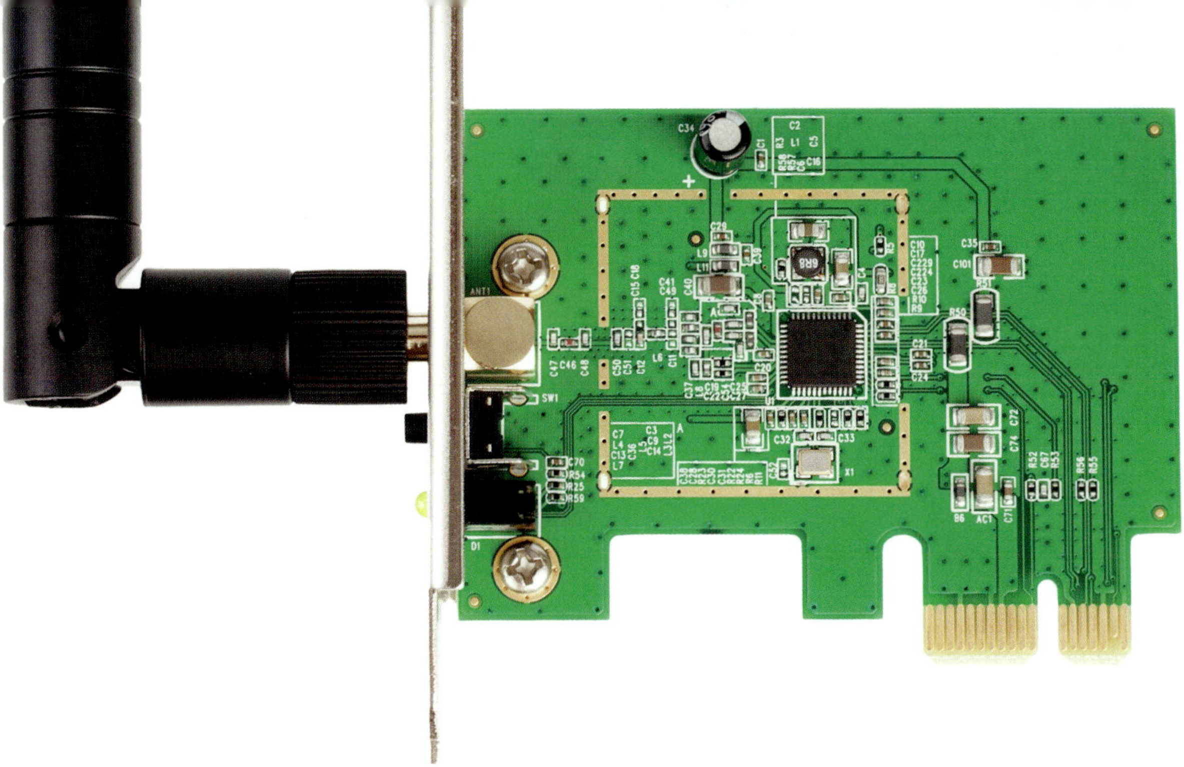

The antenna is connected to a computer chip that processes the signals.

Some Wi-Fi antennas are omnidirectional. They pick up radio waves from all directions equally well. They can send waves in all directions, too. Other Wi-Fi antennas are directional. These antennas pick up radio waves that come from one particular direction.

Wireless routers allow people to access the Internet from many points around the home.

They also send out waves in one direction. Because these antennas focus on a smaller area, they can often send the radio waves farther.

Most Wi-Fi networks work best within 150 feet (46 m) of their access point. That is approximately the width of a football field. However, this distance varies depending on the frequency, the devices used, and the environment.

CRITICAL THINKING

What are three similarities between the ways that music and Wi-Fi signals are sent and received?

FREQUENCY HOPPING

Other devices also use the junk bands. Signals sent by Wi-Fi devices must not interfere with these other devices. That is why Wi-Fi devices switch back and forth between different frequencies. This is known as frequency hopping.

A device starts using one frequency. It uses that frequency for a short period, such as one second. Then the device changes to a different frequency. It stays on that new frequency for a short time. Then it switches to a third frequency. The device will switch frequencies many times.

For frequency hopping to work, the device's transmitter and receiver must work together closely. They need to know which frequency to use. Each time the frequency changes, they must

Frequency hopping was invented in the 1940s.

go to the same new frequency. They must switch frequencies at the same time, too.

CHAPTER 4

STAYING CONNECTED

When several computers are connected together, they form a local area network (LAN). Computers that are part of a LAN can send and receive information along wires. When computers use Wi-Fi to connect, they form a wireless local area network (WLAN). In a WLAN, the information is sent over radio waves.

Some schools use Wi-Fi networks to allow students to share information in the classroom.

Computers are not the only devices that can be part of a WLAN. Devices such as smartphones and tablets often connect to Wi-Fi networks as well.

Through Wi-Fi, the devices can access the Internet. The devices can send and receive information as long as they are near a wireless access point (WAP). WAPs then connect the wireless devices to the Internet.

Data sent over the Internet is broken into small chunks called packets. A WAP's receiver picks up the packets sent by a wireless device. Most WAPs connect to the Internet using cables. They convert the packets into a format that can be sent along the cable. The WAP's transmitter sends the packets to their destination on the Internet.

A WAP can also send data from the Internet to a wireless device. It uses the same process, but in reverse.

WI-FI NETWORK

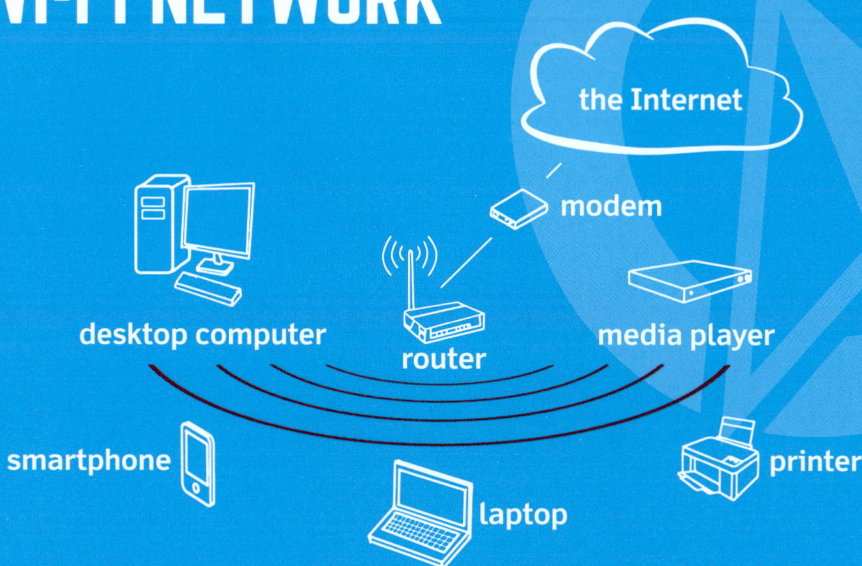

CHAPTER 5

FASTER AND STRONGER

It took less than 20 years for Wi-Fi to become common in many public places. People can even use Wi-Fi on some buses and airplanes. More and more devices have built-in Wi-Fi capabilities, too. Many video game consoles, TVs, and printers can now use Wi-Fi.

Some watches and phones can communicate with one another using Wi-Fi.

Some trains, such as this one in Germany, offer passengers Wi-Fi access.

Wi-Fi is constantly being improved. The future of Wi-Fi is all about having more and better access. This is especially true in the areas of access speed and power. Access speed continues to increase. Still, streaming movies and playing online games require a large amount of data. Sometimes a device must pause and wait for the data to be sent or received. This can be frustrating for users.

Researchers are always looking for ways to send more data more quickly. A new Wi-Fi standard uses a new frequency band, 60 gigahertz. This standard will be more than twice as fast as current Wi-Fi.

Wi-Fi devices use lots of power to send and receive radio waves. This quickly drains the device's batteries. Scientists are working on new ways to send and receive Wi-Fi signals. These techniques would use less power and give devices longer battery lives. Wi-Fi devices of the future may be even more efficient.

FOCUS ON
WI-FI

Write your answers on a separate piece of paper.

1. Write a paragraph summarizing how frequency hopping works.
2. What are some advantages of having an agency such as the FCC control who can broadcast radio waves? Can you think of any disadvantages?
3. In what year was the 802.11 standard released?
   - **A.** 1988
   - **B.** 1997
   - **C.** 1999
4. What would happen if a WAP's transmitter broke?
   - **A.** The WAP could not send data over the Internet.
   - **B.** The WAP could not convert radio waves into packets.
   - **C.** The WAP could not pick up signals from wireless devices around it.

Answer key on page 32.

GLOSSARY

broadcast
To send out radio or TV signals.

data
Information represented by numbers, especially for computers.

frequency
The number of cycles per second that a radio wave has.

gigahertz
A unit for measuring a wave's frequency that is equal to 1 billion hertz.

licenses
Formal or legal permission to do something.

megahertz
A unit for measuring a wave's frequency that is equal to 1 million hertz.

receiver
A device that picks up and converts radio waves or other signals.

standard
A set of rules made by an authority.

transmitter
A device that sends out radio waves or other signals.

TO LEARN MORE

BOOKS

Anniss, Matthew. *Understanding Computer Networks.* Chicago: Capstone Heinemann Library, 2015.

Gifford, Clive. *Computer Networks.* New York: Crabtree Publishing, 2015.

Hudak, Heather. *Waves and Information Transfer.* New York: Crabtree Publishing, 2017.

NOTE TO EDUCATORS

Visit **www.focusreaders.com** to find lesson plans, activities, links, and other resources related to this title.

INDEX

Answer Key: 1. Answers will vary; **2.** Answers will vary; **3.** B; **4.** A